This notebook belongs to:

....

To my mother, Peg Spain Murtagh, who inspired
me to be a writer, and to my sons, Connor,
Dylan, and Christopher Paratore who make me
the proudest mother in the world.
–C. M. P.

ISBN 978-1-939775-04-7

13 12 11 10   1 2 3 4 5 6 7 8 9 10

Printed in the United States of America

Little Pickle Press, Inc.
3701 Sacramento Street #494
San Francisco, CA 94118

Please visit us at www.littlepicklepress.com.

Fireflies

A Writer's Notebook

By Coleen Murtagh Paratore

Little Pickle Press

Dear Fellow Writer,

Hello and welcome to your book. I wish you much happy writing here.

Have you ever poked holes in the lid of a jar and set out to catch a firefly? As a child spending summer nights at my family's camp, I loved chasing after those mysterious and elusive "SPARKS in the dark." It was so much fun! On lucky nights I'd catch one, and for a few exciting moments, before I set it free, I would treasure that blinking star in the jar, soaking in the magic.

As an author, I can tell you that ideas are just like fireflies. You never know when they will flicker. That's what makes writing so fascinating. Ideas surprise us the same way fireflies SPARK and we must catch them, fast as we can, before they fly away.

This book will be your own special jar for catching firefly ideas. The amazing thing about thoughts is that no one else on the planet will ever have the exact same ideas with the same feelings as you, because there is only one YOU. No two people have identical experiences or memories, hurts or hopes or dreams. No one else is living your life; no one else can tell your story.

The fireflies that SPARK for you, SPARK for you and you alone. No one else can see them. Only you can catch them.

How do you catch them?

WRite them DOWN!

Write them down, write them down, write them down.

Who knows where those lights will lead you? Perhaps some will grow brighter and more interesting to you, and one day you'll set them free in a story, a speech, a play, a poem, a letter, a song, a book, or whatever form you choose.

Are you ready to open your firefly jar? Great. Your future is a blank page before you. So many good ideas are coming your way! Write what only you can write. The world is waiting to read it.

Ready . . .

Set . . .

SPARK!

"WRITING
IS
SEEING.
IT IS
PAYING
ATTENTION."

—Kate DiCamillo

HOW TO catch a firefly idea

Firefly ideas seem to come out of nowhere. You'll be living your normal life when, all of a sudden—SPARK—you'll see something or hear something or think something or feel something or remember something or imagine something, and a light will blink inside you. You will be interested. You will be inspired. When this happens, open this book and write it down.

You just caught a firefly idea. See how easy it is?

NO RULES

You can use this book whenever and however you wish. There are no rules, except to have fun and not worry about making "mistakes." There is no right or wrong way to catch firefly ideas. The important thing is to catch them before they fly away. Fireflies are fast. They don't wait around SPARKING forever.

Use a pencil, a pen, or colorful markers, or glue in text you have typed elsewhere . . . the choice is yours. You may catch a firefly idea today or tomorrow, put the book aside for a week, then get a brand-new idea and write every day for a month.

Catch the SPARKS whenever they come.

Write what you are "lit up" about.

Firefly-catching tips

Jot the day, month, and year next to your entries. This will give you a record of what you were thinking and feeling at different points in your life. Take this book with you on your travels. Make a point of leafing through it every few weeks or so. Keep this book someplace special. Hold on to it forever. One day it will be a record of who you were, how you felt, and what you were wondering about at certain ages in your life. It will be a *treasure*.

Over time you may notice that certain ideas SPARK in you again and again, sometimes months, even years, apart. These are often the ideas that ignite your most powerful writing.

Every once in a while, read over what you've written, and circle what is really lighting up for you. Then write about that.

"The scariest moment is always just before you start."

—Stephen King

FINDING the FIREFLY FIELDS

Ideas can surprise you like fireflies on a dark summer
night, but sometimes it seems like all of the fireflies are
hiding. That's when you travel to the *firefly fields*.

Where are they?

Put one hand on your head and one hand on
your heart. These are your firefly fields.

Right there, in your own mind and heart,
you have more SPARKLING ideas than you
will ever have time to write about.

Heart

On a blank page, draw a big heart. Fill it with the words for everything you *love* . . . people, places, things, feelings. Draw more hearts on more blank pages as needed. The heart is the richest source of SPARKS for your writing.

Head

On a blank page, draw the outline of a head. Fill it with the words for every-thing you know a lot about . . . topics, people, places, things, feelings. Write what you care about—write what you know about. That's the secret.

Heart

HEAD

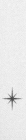

what's SParKiNG FOR you?

Read over the firefly ideas you've caught inside the heart and head and circle whatever is SPARKiNG for you . . . anything you'd be interested in writing about, excited to write about, or would enjoy writing about. Let these SParKS lead the way in choosing what to write. Catch all of the SParKS that come to you. They come to you for a reason.

....
....
....
....
....
....
....
....
....
....
....
....
....
....
....
....
....
....
....
....

SPARK
starters

While the firefly fields of your own mind and
heart hold the brightest SPARKS for igniting your
writing, sometimes you might want additional
"SPARK starters" to light your way.

If you'd like some extra inspiration,
these starters are sprinkled throughout
the book, and there are lots of blank
pages to use as you wish.

This is your book.

enjoy it!

memories

What are your most powerful memories, the moments you will never forget?
Why are they so important to you?

....
....
....
....
....
....
....
....
....
....
....
....
....
....
....
....
....
....
....
....
....
....
....
....
....

senses

The five senses are valuable tools for writers. Seeing, hearing, smelling, tasting, or touching something new or wonderful or strange can light an idea inside you.

I will always remember the sight of ....

....

....

....

....

....

....

....

I will always remember the sound of ....

....

....

....

....

....

....

....

I will always remember the smell of ....

....

....

....

....

....

....

....

....

I will always remember the taste of ....

....

....

....

....

....

....

....

I will always remember the touch of ....

....

....

....

....

....

....

....

emotions

The poet Robert Frost said, "No tears in the writer, no tears in the reader; no surprise for the writer, no surprise for the reader." When you are speaking honestly from your deepest feelings, readers will be drawn in and want to read on.

I was so happy when ....
....
....
....
....

I was so sad when ....
....
....
....
....

I was so excited when ....
....
....
....
....

I was so embarrassed when ....
....
....
....
....

I laughed so hard when ....

....

....

....

....

I was so scared when ....

....

....

....

....

I was so angry when ....

....

....

....

....

I was so disappointed when ....

....

....

....

....

I was so proud when ....

....

....

....

....

I was so surprised when ....

....

....

....

....

I was so jealous when ....

....

....

....

....

I felt so peaceful when ....

....

....

....

....

I felt so safe and secure when ....

....

....

....

....

I felt so loved when ....

....

....

....

....

I felt so helpless when ....

....

....

....

....

I felt so strong when ....

....

....

....

....

I felt so lonely when ....

....

....

....

....

I felt so included and part of a group when ....

....

....

....

....

I felt so joyful when ....

....

....

....

....

teachers

Write about a teacher you will never forget. Is there a specific example or story you remember?

....
....
....
....
....
....
....
....
....
....
....
....
....
....
....
....
....
....
....
....
....
....

FREEWRITING

Open to a blank page
and, starting at the top, write whatever
you are hearing in your head. Write as fast
as you can, not stopping for a second,
not worrying about spelling or punctuation,
just writing as freely as you can all the
way to the bottom of the page.
When you are done, read it over.
Circle anything that is SPARKING for you.
Now write about that.

DREAMS

Sometimes you wake up and remember a dream.
Write down those that interest you.

....
....
....
....
....
....
....
....
....
....
....
....
....
....
....
....
....
....
....
....
....
....
....

FRee aLL yeaR

What do you love that is free?
See how many things you can think of!

....

....

....

....

....

....

....

....

....

....

....

....

....

....

....

....

....

....

....

....

....

....

....

WRITTEN TREASURES

Are there things people have written to you, for you, or about you that you will always treasure? Are there things you have written to, for, or about someone else that you remember?

IDEA:

You might paste an envelope inside the back cover of this book to keep mementos that inspire you such as special cards, letters, event programs, or ticket stubs.

curiosities

What are you curious about? What would you like to learn about?

....
....
....
....
....
....
....
....
....
....
....
....
....
....
....
....
....
....
....
....
....
....

pets

Write about pets, past or present, or the pet you wish you could have.

First & Last Times

The "first times" and "last times" in life are rich sources of writing topics.

I'll always remember the first time ....

....

....

....

....

....

....

....

....

....

....

....

....

....

....

....

....

....

....

....

....

....

....

....

I'll always remember the last time ....

....

....

....

....

....

....

....

....

....

....

....

....

....

....

....

....

....

....

....

....

....

....

....

....

"Love the
writing,
Love the
writing,
Love the
writing.
the rest
will follow."

—Jane Yolen

major milestones

If you were to write your life story, what would be the highlights so far?

....
....
....
....
....
....
....
....
....
....
....
....
....
....
....
....
....
....
....
....
....
....
....

write yourself "right"

I find that in the most difficult times of my life, if I pick up a pen and just pour out all of the pain onto the page, I feel so much better, and often more hopeful. When things are hard, try writing yourself "right."

....

....

....

....

....

....

....

....

....

....

....

....

....

....

....

....

....

....

....

....

Happy Birthday to you

Your birthday is your own special holiday, the start of a brand-new year for you. Take a few minutes each year on your birthday to write a note to yourself. What is life like for you right now? Who and what is important to you? What are your wishes for the next year?

....

....

....

....

....

....

....

....

....

....

....

....

....

....

....

....

....

....

HOLiDAYS & VACATiONS

Write about the best and worst holidays or vacations ever.

....
....
....
....
....
....
....
....
....
....
....
....
....
....
....
....
....
....
....
....
....
....
....
....

TOP-TEN Lists

Start lists of your favorite things. For example: books, movies, songs, places, etc.

Births & Deaths

Write about the births or deaths of people in your life.

....
....
....
....
....
....
....
....
....
....
....
....
....
....
....
....
....
....
....
....
....
....
....
....
....
....

HELLOS & GOOD-BYES

Write about the first time you met someone who is important to you, or a good-bye you will never forget.

....
....
....
....
....
....
....
....
....
....
....
....
....
....
....
....
....
....
....
....
....
....
....

Nature

Go outside for a walk and notice nature. Write about what you experience.

....
....
....
....
....
....
....
....
....
....
....
....
....
....
....
....
....
....
....
....
....
....

secret hideout

Do you have a favorite place you like to go? Did you have a secret hideout when you were younger?

....
....
....
....
....
....
....
....
....
....
....
....
....
....
....
....
....
....
....
....
....
....

"WRITE as
much as you
WANT AND tell
everything and
put it all on
the page.
Then rewrite it."

—Jacqueline Woodson

FiNDiNG YOUR VOiCE

If there is something in the news that makes you angry, sad, proud, or deter-
mined to speak out and make your voice heard, write it down. What are some
issues or causes that you feel strongly about? If you were in charge, how would
you make things better? Is there a letter you would like to write to your principal,
the local newspaper, your town's mayor, a senator, or perhaps the president?

....
....
....
....
....
....
....
....
....
....
....
....
....
....
....
....
....

WISDOM

Has a parent, grandparent, or other loved one taught you a wise life lesson?

....

....

....

....

....

....

....

....

TO DO

You may have something important to accomplish and you're not sure where to begin. Start by making a "To Do" list, jotting down small steps that will move you forward.

....

....

....

....

....

....

....

....

TRADITIONS

Write about your favorite family traditions.

....
....
....
....
....
....
....
....
....
....
....
....
....
....
....
....
....
....
....
....
....
....
....
....

PROS & CONS

When you're trying to make a decision, sometimes it helps to draw a line down the center of a blank page. Label one side Pros (positive points) and the other side Cons (negative points) and write down all of the things that come to mind.

....
....
....
....
....
....
....
....
....
....
....
....
....
....
....
....
....
....
....
....
....
....
....
....
....
....
....

INSPIRING QUOTES

The walls of my writing studio are covered with quotes that inspire me. Use this page to write down your favorite lines from books, movies, or anything that makes you happy or encourages you.

a GROCERY List

If you are struggling with starting a writing project, don't put a lot of pressure on yourself to write in perfect sentences, one after another. Just make a grocery list to start. Jot down anything that might be an ingredient: a word, phrase, question, or whatever you think of that might get included in the final recipe.

....
....
....
....
....
....
....
....
....
....
....
....
....
....
....
....
....
....
....
....
....

ONE THING

You may have lots of ideas for things to write about. If you had to choose *the one thing* you feel most called to write about, what would it be? Write that.

....
....
....
....
....
....
....
....
....
....
....
....
....
....
....
....
....
....
....
....
....
....
....

"make your
own rules.
or,
better yet,
have
no rules."

~Karen Cushman

TaKE a TRiP

Go somewhere! Even a walk to the corner can SPaRK firefly ideas if you pay close attention to whatever catches your eye. When you get home, write about what you saw and heard or who you met along the way.

....
....
....
....
....
....
....
....
....
....
....
....
....
....
....
....
....
....
....
....
....

HiGHS & LOWS

What was the best part of your day? The worst part?

....
....
....
....
....
....
....
....
....
....
....
....
....
....
....
....
....
....
....
....
....
....
....
....
....
....

HAPPY

What makes you happy?

....
....
....
....
....
....
....
....
....
....
....
....
....
....
....
....
....
....
....
....
....
....
....

TRUE

What do you know to be absolutely true in life?

....
....
....
....
....
....
....
....
....
....
....
....
....
....
....
....
....
....
....
....
....
....
....

your gifts

We are all born with special gifts to give the world. What are yours?

....
....
....
....
....
....
....
....
....
....
....
....
....
....
....
....
....
....
....
....
....
....
....
....
....

your future

What dreams do you have for yourself, for your future?

....
....
....
....
....
....
....
....
....
....
....
....
....
....
....
....
....
....
....
....
....
....
....
....
....
....
....
....

KEEP ON
WRITING . . .

Ideas are like fireflies. They like to surprise us.
The best ideas, the brightest SPARKS,
are in the blinking-twinkling firefly
fields of your own mind and heart.
Return there again and again and
you will always be amazed.

SPARK
SPARK
SPARK!

Enjoy!

OUR MISSION

Little Pickle Press is
dedicated to helping
parents and educators
cultivate conscious,
responsible little people
by stimulating explorations
of the meaningful topics
of their generation
through a variety of
media, technologies,
and techniques.

Little Pickle Press
Environmental Benefits Statement

This book is printed on International Paper's Accent Vellum Opaque.
It is made with 10% PCRF (Post-Consumer Recovered Fiber),
is FSC®-certified, and an acid-free paper.

Little Pickle Press saved the following resources by using U2:XG paper:

.rees	energy	greenhouse gases	wastewater	solid waste
onsumer red fiber es wood th savings ed as trees.	PCRF content displaces energy used to process equivalent virgin fiber.	Measured in CO_2 equivalents, PCRF content and Green Power reduce greenhouse gas emissions.	PCRF content eliminates wastewater needed to process equivalent virgin fiber.	PCRF content eliminates solid waste generated by producing an equivalent amount of virgin fiber through the pulp and paper manufacturing process.
trees	3 mil BTUs	693 lbs	3,716 gal	252 lbs

Calculations based on research by Environmental Defense Fund and other members
of the Paper Task Force and applies to print quanities of 7,500 books.

B Corporations are a new type of company that use the power of business to solve social
and environmental problems. Little Pickle Press is proud to be a Certified B Corporation.

www.littlepicklepress.com

author's note

When my first books were published and I began visiting schools to talk about writing, I used a yellow-topped plastic jar purchased at a dollar store to illustrate how when ideas surprise us like fireflies on a summer night, we must catch them fast as we can. In 2006, at Hamagrael Elementary in Delmar, New York, a boy named Udeep Bassi ran up to me excitedly and said, "You should write about the fireflies!" That was nearly a decade ago, and I still use that same yellow-topped jar. Now each year countless children write to tell me about their "firefly ideas" and what they are writing about. These letters bring me such joy and inspire me greatly.

about the author

A full-time writer and teacher of writing, Coleen Murtagh Paratore is the author of eighteen titles, spanning picture books through young adult novels, including the award-winning, *BIG*, the best-selling *The Wedding Planner's Daughter*, which sparked the popular series about Willa Havisham, a girl who wants to be a writer, the critically-acclaimed *Sunny Holiday*, and the autobiographical novel, *Dreamsleeves*. Coleen loves to encourage and inspire writers of all ages. She teaches at Russell Sage College and The Arts Center of the Capital Region, and presents at conferences, libraries, and schools throughout the country where she always brings the same yellow-topped jar, talks about "catching the fireflies sparking in your own mind and heart," and gets every person in the room writing, writing, writing. The mother of three wonderful sons, Coleen lives in Troy, New York. For information on her books or to schedule an appearance, visit her at www.coleenparatore.com.

"catch ideas
like fireflies
on a summer
night,
and write
what only
you can
write."

—Coleen Paratore